Pt-3

This book is to be returned on or before the last date stamped below.

READING COLLECTION

F
DUN

Falkirk Council

To The Very Kind
John, Mary and Miriam Kiki
J.D.

For Rowan,
My Very Big
D.G.

THE VERY SMALL
A PICTURE CORGI BOOK : 0 552 546437

First published in Great Britain by Doubleday, a division of Transworld Publishers

PRINTING HISTORY
Doubleday edition published 2000
Picture Corgi edition published 2001

3 5 7 9 10 8 6 4 2

Text copyright © Joyce Dunbar, 2000
Illustrations copyright © Debi Gliori, 2000

Designed by Ian Butterworth

The right of Joyce Dunbar to be identified as the author and of Debi Gliori as the illustrator of this
work has been asserted in accordance with the Copyright, Designs and Patents Act 1988

Picture Corgi Books are published by Transworld Publishers,
61-63 Uxbridge Road, London W5 5SA,
a division of The Random House Group Ltd,
in Australia by Random House Australia (Pty) Ltd,
20 Alfred Street, Milsons Point, Sydney, NSW 2061,
in New Zealand by Random House New Zealand Ltd,
18 Poland Road, Glenfield, Auckland 10,
and in South Africa by Random House (Pty) Ltd,
Endulini, 5A Jubilee Road, Parktown 2193

Printed in Singapore

www.booksattransworld.co.uk/childrens

The Very Small

Joyce Dunbar

Illustrated by

Debi Gliori

PICTURE CORGI BOOKS

One day, when Giant Baby Bear
was playing in the woods, he found a very small...

...something!

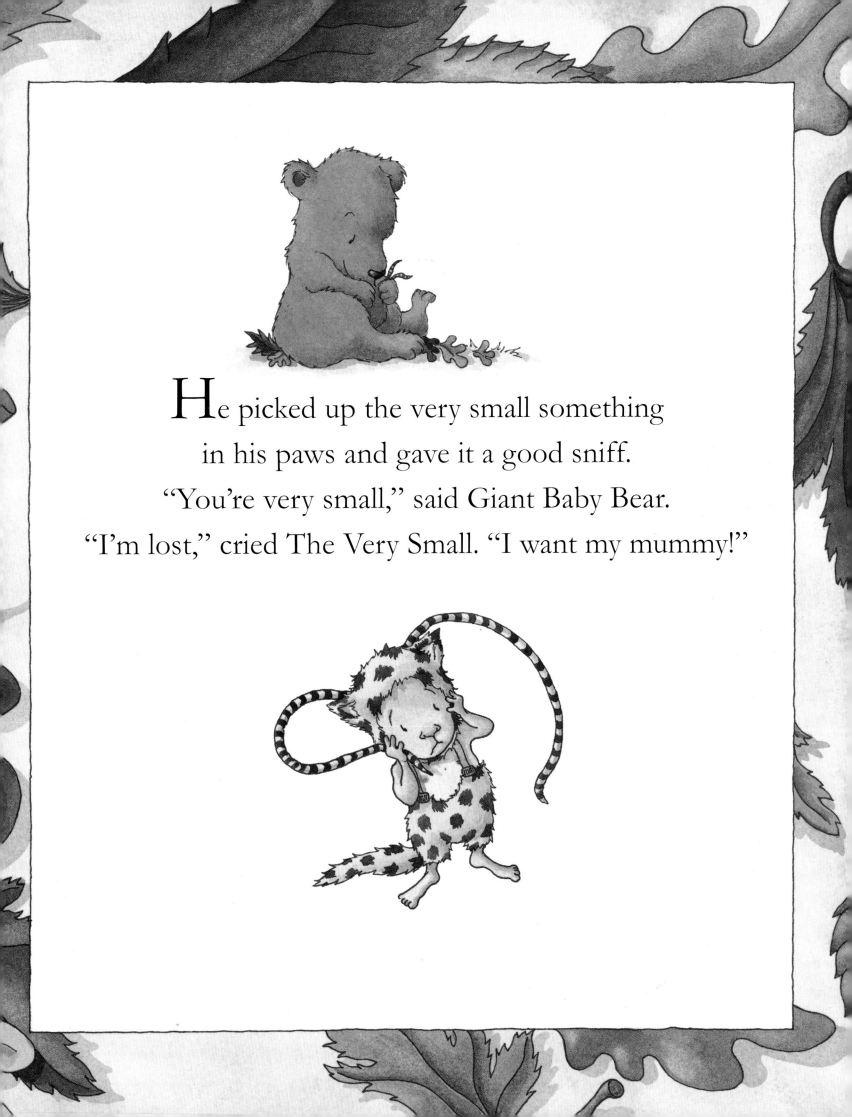

He picked up the very small something
in his paws and gave it a good sniff.
"You're very small," said Giant Baby Bear.
"I'm lost," cried The Very Small. "I want my mummy!"

"I don't know where your mummy is,"
said Giant Baby Bear,
"but you can share my mummy if you like."
And he took The Very Small home to his mother
and placed it in one of her very large paws.
His mother gave a great big grin
showing all her great big teeth.
"What's this you've found?"
said Giant Mummy Bear.

"I want my daddy!" howled The Very Small.

"I don't know where your daddy is,"
said Giant Baby Bear,
"but you can share my daddy if you like."
And Giant Baby Bear took The Very Small from his
mummy's very large paws and placed him in
his daddy's even larger paws.
Giant Daddy Bear stared hard through his spectacles.
"What's this you've found?" he growled.

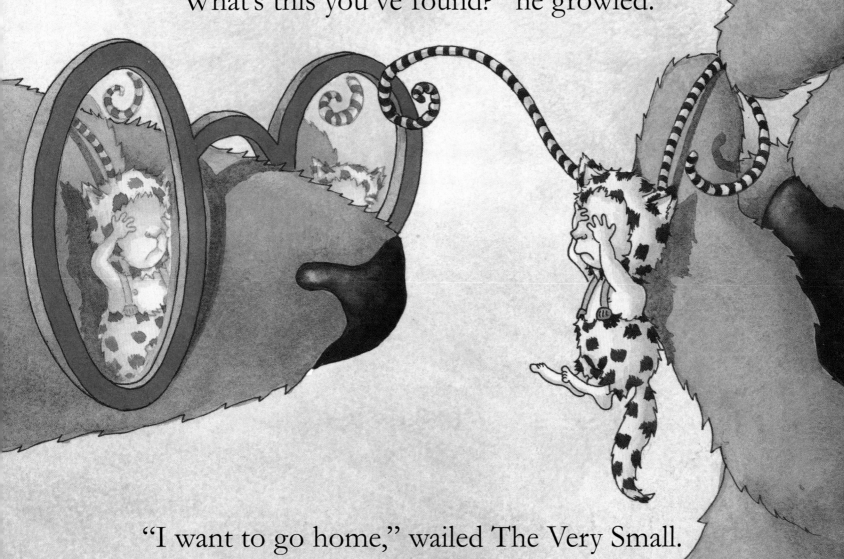

"I want to go home," wailed The Very Small.

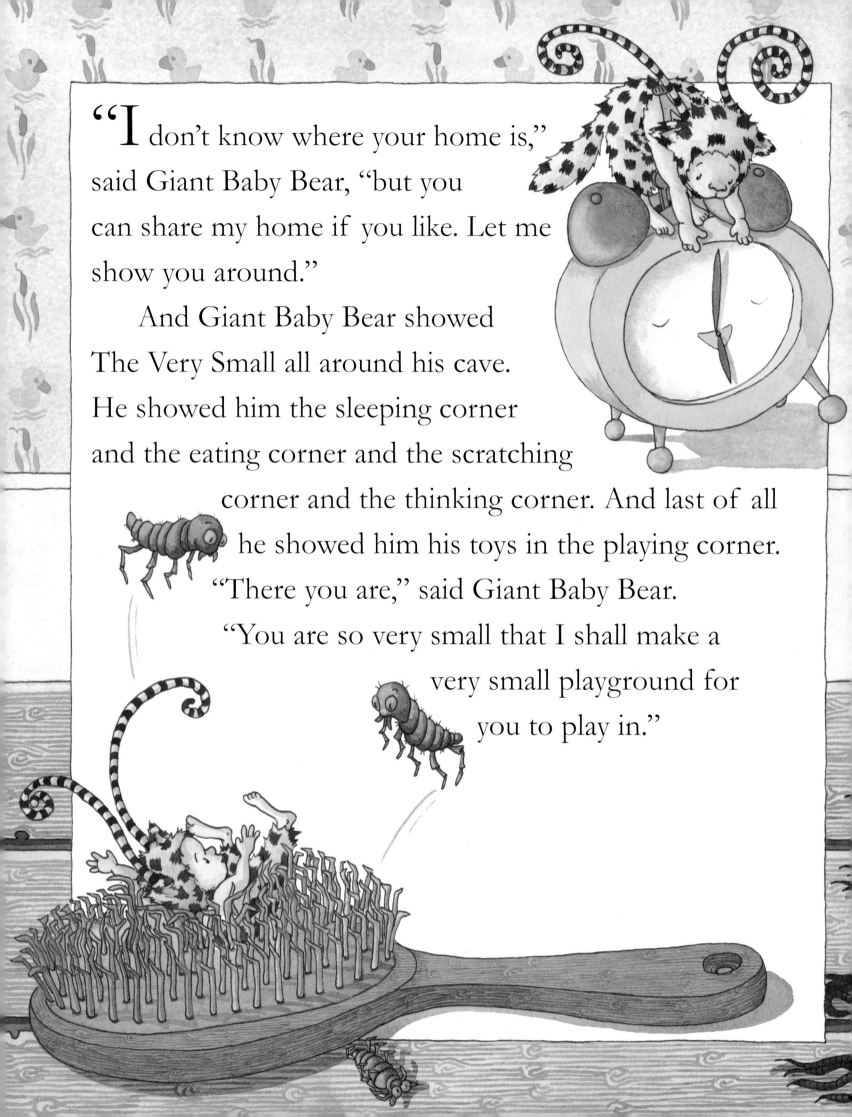

"I don't know where your home is,"
said Giant Baby Bear, "but you
can share my home if you like. Let me
show you around."

And Giant Baby Bear showed
The Very Small all around his cave.
He showed him the sleeping corner
and the eating corner and the scratching
corner and the thinking corner. And last of all
he showed him his toys in the playing corner.
"There you are," said Giant Baby Bear.
"You are so very small that I shall make a
very small playground for
you to play in."

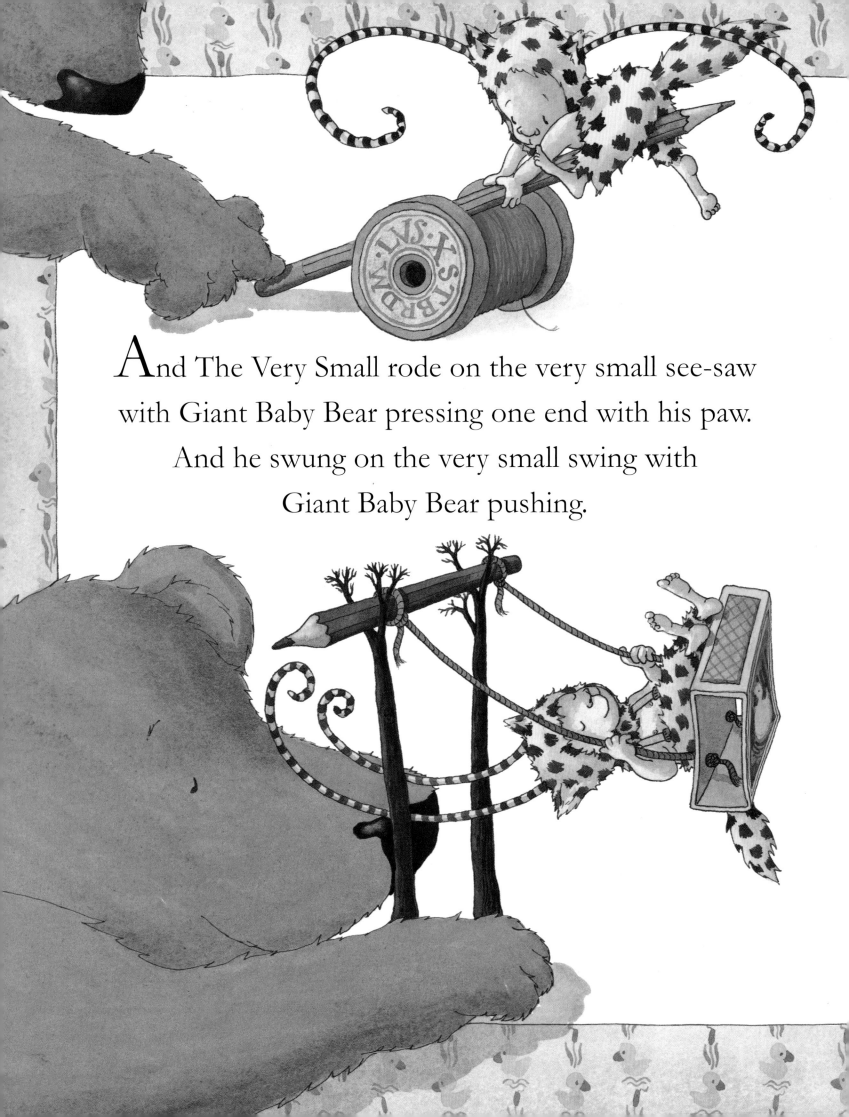

And The Very Small rode on the very small see-saw
with Giant Baby Bear pressing one end with his paw.
And he swung on the very small swing with
Giant Baby Bear pushing.

And he slid on the very small slide with Giant Baby Bear catching him in his paws.

And suddenly he felt very hungry.

"I want my dinner!" called The Very Small.

"I don't know what you were going to have for your dinner," said Giant Baby Bear,
"but you can share my dinner if you like."
And Giant Baby Bear placed The Very Small next to his plate, and The Very Small ate one whole pea and five whole crumbs of bread and he drank a whole spoonful of milk.

And then he felt very tired.
"I want my bed," said The Very Small.
"I want my bed too," said Giant Baby Bear,
"but first of all we have a bath."
And Giant Baby Bear had a splashing bath
in a great big tub, while The Very Small had
a floating bath in the soapdish.

Then Giant Baby Bear put The Very Small
right next to him on his pillow and fell asleep.
But The Very Small didn't fall asleep. Giant Baby Bear
was snoring so loudly that he couldn't.
So he pinched Giant Baby Bear's nose to try to
stop him snoring, but to Giant Baby Bear it felt very much
like a tickle and suddenly he went

...blowing The Very Small right out of the cave and across the yard and over th

...eetops until he landed in the very same part of the woods where he had got lost in the first place!

And there, waiting for him, were The Very Small's very own mummy and daddy. They were so pleased to see him. They took him home and tucked him up in his very own bed with his very own bear who suddenly seemed...

Very Small!